Look out for more adventures from

Collect them all!

1 ☐ **DRAGON RIDER**
2 ☐ **SELKIE WARRIOR**

☐ **THE DEEP: THE OFFICIAL HANDBOOK**
☐ **THE DEEP: STICKER ACTIVITY BOOK**

SELKIE WARRIOR

FINN BLACK

BLOOMSBURY
CHILDREN'S BOOKS
LONDON   OXFORD   NEW YORK   NEW DELHI   SYDNEY

With special thanks to Speckled Pen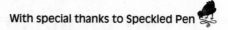

BLOOMSBURY CHILDREN'S BOOKS
Bloomsbury Publishing Plc
50 Bedford Square, London WC1B 3DP, UK

BLOOMSBURY, BLOOMSBURY CHILDREN'S BOOKS and the Diana logo
are trademarks of Bloomsbury Publishing Plc

First published in Great Britain in 2018 by Bloomsbury Publishing Plc

These books are based on the multi-award-winning television series THE DEEP,
produced by DHX Media and A Stark Production. Technicolor Creative Services
is the primary rights holder. THE DEEP series is based on the original
graphic novels created by Tom Taylor and James Brouwer

A catalogue record for this book is available from the British Library

ISBN: PB: 978-1-4088-9875-8; eBook: 978-1-4088-9876-5

2 4 6 8 10 9 7 5 3 1

Printed and bound in Great Britain by CPI Group (UK) Ltd, Croydon CR0 4YY

MIX
Paper from
responsible sources
FSC® C020471

To find out more about our authors and books visit www.bloomsbury.com
and sign up for our newsletters

With special thanks to Brandon Robshaw and David Shephard,
along with Steven Wendland and Marty Kossoff.

With additional thanks to Alison Warner, Pam Kunick-Cohen,
Avrill Stark, Robert Chandler, Tom Taylor, James Brouwer,
Wolfgang Bylsma, Trent Carlson, Kirsten Newlands, Anne Loi,
Rob Spindley, Logan McPherson, Sophie Bloomfield,
and John Lomas-Bullivant.

PROLOGUE

A tall, burly man walked with a rolling gait to the edge of the harbour. The brass buttons on his pea coat glittered in the rays of the setting sun. Waves broke gently against the sea wall, and a fishing boat bobbed in the water next to a landing stage.

Two people in overalls were crouched over the boat. One was attaching some sort of device to the front of the vessel. The other wore a welder's mask and was soldering two large metal plates together. A shower of sparks flew from the torch.

'Ahoy there!' called the burly man.

The figure in the mask straightened up and looked round sharply. A hand went up to raise the mask, revealing the face of a young woman with flushed cheeks, short dark hair and intense green eyes.

'Captain Hammerhead. About time.' The young woman climbed a set of iron steps to where the pirate stood. He gazed down at the boat. The other worker was still busily fixing some piece of tech to the prow. 'Making some improvements, Edwina?'

Edwina shrugged. 'When you don't have the Worldwide Oceanic Authority behind you, you have to be resourceful, right?'

Captain Hammerhead gave a hoarse, guttural laugh. 'You said it. Ducking and diving, that's us.' His laughter stopped as quickly as it had begun and he fixed her with a level stare. 'Got the necessary?'

Edwina delved into her pocket and brought out a grubby envelope. Captain Hammerhead snatched it and ripped it open, riffling his thumb through the notes of money inside. 'Seems to be all there,' he grunted.

'Now hand over the goods,' said Edwina. 'And this better be worth it.'

The Dark Orca's captain laughed. 'Oh, it's worth it, all right.' He took a small electronic tablet from inside his coat, touched the screen and showed her the display.

There was an image of a tarnished brown orb, small enough to fit perfectly in the palm of her hand. Around its centre was a protruding ring covered in mysterious symbols. It looked indescribably old.

Edwina snatched the tablet and stared. 'The Esgis! I thought it was lost forever!'

'Well, it ain't. It was aboard my sub not long

ago. But I never got my hands on it.'

Edwina looked up at him, eyes burning. 'Who has it, then?'

'The Nektons. They've got it on board the Aronnax. You're the only one who knows, apart from me.'

Edwina handed back the tablet and called down to the man who was still working on the boat. 'Hurry up and finish installing that, d'you hear? I need that boat, and fast.' She turned back to the captain. 'Where are the Nektons now?'

Captain Hammerhead held out a hand. 'Extra information costs money.'

Edwina narrowed her eyes. 'You've had everything you're getting.'

He grinned, revealing pearly white teeth. 'Can't blame a pirate for trying. All right, we intercepted their signal. They're headed for the Arafura Sea.'

Edwina gave a sudden high-pitched laugh.

'Good – not too far from here. I hear there's a cyclone heading that way. I can use it to my advantage.' She took out a tablet of her own and keyed in a code, her fingers a blur. Then, with an air of triumph, she held out the screen to the captain. He saw the WOA logo and underneath it the words: SATELLITE FEED TO ARONNAX – STRICTLY CONFIDENTIAL.

'I've hacked into the WOA feed – now I can intercept their messages. The Nektons won't be getting any warnings about the cyclone!'

'So they're heading straight into the storm?'

'And I'm going after them,' Edwina said, gazing out to sea.

Captain Hammerhead gave a low, appreciative whistle. 'Ain't no stoppin' you, is there?'

'I'd do anything to get hold of the Esgis,' she said, leaping down to the boat. *Anything!*

CHAPTER ONE

Ant peeled the wrapping from the fortune cookie and snapped it open. A shower of crumbs fell on the table as he pulled out the slip of paper.

'"Today is the day to show someone you care,"' he read out loud. 'Yeah, maybe there's something in that. Maybe I should show my feelings more.'

He began to walk towards his big sister,

Fontaine, arms spread wide, mouth puckered up for a kiss.

'No way – urgh!' Fontaine scampered round to the other side of the table. 'Keep away from me!'

Ant carried on walking straight past her and picked up the Jorange – the portable tank that his pet fish, Jeffrey, swam around in. He planted a kiss on the side of the fish tank, and Jeffrey swam up, and appeared to press his tiny lips to the glass.

'Thank goodness for that!' said Fontaine. 'Like, narrow escape.'

'It wasn't that narrow,' Ant assured her.

'Ha ha, very funny,' said Fontaine, folding her arms. 'Anyway, the fortune cookie said show *someone* you care. Jeffrey isn't a person, he's just ... well, just a fish!"

Ant clamped his hands to the sides of the tank. 'Hey, watch what you're saying, Jeffrey has feelings, you know! He's not *just*

anything – he's the best fish in the whole wide ocean!' He gazed down at his tiny friend. 'Aren't you, Jeffrey?'

'He's not in the ocean, he's in your home-made aquarium,' said Fontaine. 'He may be the best fish in there. Just about.'

Ant glared at Fontaine as his parents, Will and Kaiko, exchanged a smile. The Nekton family were gathered on the bridge of the Aronnax as it powered its way through the ocean. Kaiko had steered it down to a depth of a thousand metres, heading towards the Arafura Sea. They had stopped off at Hong Kong to refuel and replenish their supplies, and Ant had taken the opportunity to stock up on fortune cookies. Big time. The table was littered with cookie crumbs and empty wrappers, and there was still a sizeable pyramid of unopened cookies, containing slivers of paper waiting to tell their fortunes.

'Go on, your turn,' Ant said.

'Oh, all right.' Fontaine unwrapped another cookie, broke it apart and unfolded the message. '"Life's journey is always an adventure,"' she read aloud.

'They got that right!' said Kaiko, looking up from the screen on her console. 'I don't know how or why this happened but – our satellite connection is down!'

'I don't call that an adventure!' Ant said. 'An adventure should have, like, sharks and dragons and pirates and sea monsters!'

'Maybe they'll put in an appearance later,' said Kaiko. 'But right now this is quite enough to deal with.'

'Is it such a big deal though?' Will asked in a reassuring voice. He leaned over her to take a look at the screen. 'We can still manage – we have the charts, and you're a great pilot, Kaiko.'

A soft bleeping noise, like someone hitting a xylophone with a padded stick, rang through the bridge. 'Ah, that means we've entered a new area. We're in the Celebes Sea now,' Kaiko said.

Will pored over one of his charts on the map table. 'Just under five hundred kilometres till we hit the Arafura Sea.'

'Arafura,' Ant said dreamily. 'Isn't that a great name? "Child of the Mountain", that's what it means.'

'Yeah, but what does *that* mean?' said Fontaine. 'Does anybody know?'

Will looked up, a curious frown on his face.

'I don't know yet,' said Ant. 'But I'll find out. Mysteries are made to be solved!'

He went over to the display stand on the map table, where the Ephemychron lived. Once a navigational tool of the ancient Lemurian people, it was a greenish copper orb covered with mysterious symbols. Beside the Ephemychron stood another, smaller orb of tarnished brown. The Circlotron. Together, they looked like a planet and its moon, thought Ant. The Circlotron had a ring around its middle, covered in more Lemurian etchings. Ant had discovered it during a dive in a kelp forest, and had lovingly restored it.

He'd found a way of switching on the Circlotron so that it shot a beam of light into the night sky, picking out the celestial equator. The first time it had happened was so cool! Admittedly, Ant still wasn't quite sure what the device was actually *for*, but he had an idea that it was tracing a route. A route that the Nektons were supposed to follow. To where ... ? It was Ant's mission to find out.

He carefully took the Circlotron from its holder on the map table. It was the size of a cricket ball – small enough to balance in the palm of his hand. He often placed it inside his Jorange, so he could take it on his travels if needed. Plus Jeffrey was a great guard-fish.

Now he held the Circlotron in his hands. He was the only person who could control it and when he held it, a beam of light would shoot out. There were other times when some of the etchings on the rim had lit up. The etching of the dragon had taken them to a lair where Ant had found a hidden cave. There, another symbol had lit up on the Circlotron – of a child and mountain. It matched a symbol carved into the cave and Ant felt certain the Circlotron was guiding them along the equator towards the Arafura Sea, named after the Child of the Mountain.

'Not now, Ant!' said his mother, as if she had eyes in the back of her head. 'I'm trying to navigate and I don't want beams of light shooting all over the bridge, thank you very much!' She peered more closely at the screen in front of her. 'Something funny's going on here. Looks like there's an object – what is it, a fish? – moving about under the hull.'

Will came to stand beside her. 'Pretty big fish,' he commented.

'Oh wow, d'you think it's a great white shark?' said Ant excitedly. 'Or a giant oarfish? Or ... or ... ?'

'Calm down, Ant,' Kaiko said. 'I can't get a proper look at it. It's too close to the hull.'

Ant came running over to the console and squeezed in beside his mother. Fontaine followed. A dark, blurred shape was moving on the screen. It grew bigger and the next moment there was a *bump* that rocked the Aronnax.

'It hit us!' said Fontaine.

'Whatever creature's down there, it's a bold one,' Will said.

'Maybe it's a sea serpent!' Ant said. He just couldn't stop imagining sea creatures. 'Or ... or ... a sea goat!'

'A *what*?' said Fontaine, giving him a withering glance.

'A sea goat – I've been studying the stars. Did you know there's a whole constellation named after the sea goat – Capricornus!'

'Yes, Ant, but it's not an actual creature,' Fontaine said patiently. 'I suppose you'll be saying there's a giant scorpion in the sea next, just because there's a constellation named after that.'

'Who knows what's down there in the deep?' Ant challenged her. 'We didn't expect to find a dragon – until we found one.'

'It was an evolved plesiosaur, not a dragon,' said Fontaine.

'Well, we didn't expect to find a plesiosaur!' They'd encountered the ancient creature living in a cave at the blue hole in the South China Sea. Ant had even ridden on its back. He was so excited, he'd christened the ancient creature – um – Brian.

'Anyway, we didn't expect to find Brian,

but we did!' he reminded his sister. She wasn't going to win this argument!

Before Fontaine could reply there was another *bump*. The ship lurched more violently than before. Kaiko and Will exchanged a concerned look.

'Do you think we should go out and chase it away, whatever it is?' said Will.

'I'm sure it doesn't mean to harm us,' Kaiko said, sounding less than one hundred per cent sure. Then she brightened. 'Anyway, look, it's going!'

Sure enough, the shape on the screen was getting smaller.

Ant ran to the window and peered out into the ocean, hoping to catch a glimpse of the creature. He thought he saw a black, streamlined shape moving swiftly away from the Aronnax – but before he could focus on it properly, it had disappeared.

'Whew,' said Will. 'Alarm over.'

Kaiko shook out her shoulders and stretched her neck. 'You guys can take a break if you like. We're on course, and everything's under control now.'

'Sure?'

'I know you've been dying to go to your library and consult your books, ever since Fontaine asked Ant why the Arafura Sea is called Child of the Mountain!'

Will grinned. 'Am I really that transparent?' He was already walking towards the library.

Ant and Fontaine followed. Ant wondered what idea had occurred to his dad. Perhaps he'd suddenly remembered something buried in one of his old books, another clue that would guide them in their quest to understand the mysteries of the ancient Lemurians!

CHAPTER TWO

The library aboard the Aronnax looked like it belonged either in a university or a museum. It was a strange mix of the old and the ultra-modern. There were bookcases full of ancient leather-bound books and maps and atlases. There was a painted wooden globe, fashioned in the seventeenth century, which showed the continents with slightly different outlines from the ones Ant knew, and different place names, like Siam instead of Thailand and Cathay instead of China. But there were also computers and monitors, an electronic catalogue and a high-definition screen that showed the Aronnax's swift progress across a 3-D map of the ocean.

Will settled at his desk and put his glasses on. He reached up to a shelf above the desk and pulled down a large scroll wound around a stone cylinder.

'Do you think the answer will be in *The Chronicle of the Deep*, Dad?' asked Ant.

'I often find this is the best place to uncover ancient secrets, apart from the Deep itself,' Will murmured.

He opened the protective plates, unfurled the scroll inside and flattened it on the desk. The scroll was covered in pictures, diagrams, symbols and incomprehensible script in faded greys and greens and yellows. Ant and Fontaine waited patiently until their dad found what he was looking for.

'Ah! Look!' He jabbed his finger at a central symbol. It was the same image Ant had seen on the Circlotron, the stick-figure child beside the mountain. Underneath was some writing – Lemurian, Ant knew, although he couldn't read it.

'What does it say?' he asked, his foot tapping with excitement.

Will scratched his jaw, and said in his slow, deep voice, 'King Batu.'

'Who was he?' said Ant.

Will shook his head. 'I don't know.'

'So we're none the wiser!' said Fontaine.

'Not yet,' Will said, 'but –'

The muffled bleep rang out again, and looking up at the big screen Ant saw the shape of the Aronnax nosing into an area of lighter green on the map, marked ARAFURA SEA. At the same time, Kaiko's voice called out, 'We've arrived!'

'Ah,' said Will. 'Let's go and see what's what.'
He replaced the scroll on the shelf as Ant and
Fontaine raced back to the bridge.

*

All four of the Nektons stood in front of the
main window. The ocean was the colour of jade,
a paler green than they were used to – the
Celebes Sea had been almost black.

'How come the water's so much lighter?'
asked Ant.

'We're not as deep as we were,' Will said.
'The Arafura is a shallow sea.'

'I guess that means there's less sea to
search,' Fontaine said. 'But what are we looking
for?'

They'd come here, following a sign from
the Circlotron. They'd decided that the
etching of the stick-figure child beside the
mountain meant that they should come to the
Arafura Sea – especially after the beam of light
had arced west in the night sky, pointing to

a spot above the ocean right here. They had to be in the right place, Ant felt sure of that. Still, he had to admit Fontaine had a point. They didn't know exactly what they were searching for.

'We'll know when we find it,' Will said.

'Yeah,' said Ant, determined to stay positive. This was one of the most exciting things to happen to him, ever. He wasn't going to let a small detail like the Nektons having No Actual Plan put him off. 'This is where the Circlotron led us – so there's got to be *something* here.'

A high-pitched keening sound suddenly burst out, making Ant and Fontaine jump.

Fontaine put her hands to her ears. 'What's that horrible noise?'

'Sounds a like a seagull that's stubbed its toe really badly!' said Ant.

'It's the distress signal,' said Kaiko, whirling round. 'Someone's in trouble!'

'Can't you turn it down?' said Fontaine, her hands still over her ears.

Will moved over to one of the computers. He touched the monitor screen and a set of coordinates appeared, along with the letters SOS repeated over and over again. 'It's coming from a boat on the surface, not too far from here.'

'Sounds like a job for the Nektons!' said Ant.

'I'll take us up,' said Kaiko. She pressed a button on the console in front of her.

'*Please*, Dad!' said Fontaine. 'I have sensitive ears!'

'Oh yes, sorry.' Will grinned as he turned off the distress signal. Silence descended once more on the bridge of the Aronnax – or not quite, as there was now a rushing sound as water was pumped from the ballast tanks. As the Aronnax began to rise, the sea grew paler.

A few moments later, the mighty submarine

broke the surface. It was an overcast day with dark, bloated clouds hanging low in the sky. Heavy rain fell, splashing on the Aronnax's glass roof.

'Eyes peeled, everyone,' said Will. 'Look out for that boat!'

The bridge of the Aronnax was glass-walled, but Ant couldn't see any sign of a vessel. The sky was so dark it was hard to pick anything out. The rain was falling harder, huge raindrops bouncing off the glass, and the sky seemed to be getting darker by the moment.

'Looks like we've arrived in the middle of a storm,' Will said. 'Could be a bad one.'

'A very bad one,' Kaiko replied. She was looking at the reading on the console's electronic barometer. 'The atmospheric pressure is dropping. It's below a hundred millibars –'

The rain stopped abruptly. An eerie silence fell on the bridge of the Aronnax.

'Uh-oh,' said Will. He pointed at the barometer. The needle was now rising. Fast.

'Uh-oh,' echoed Kaiko.

'Why is everyone saying "uh-oh"?' said Ant.

Then two things happened at exactly the same moment.

An almighty crash shook the Aronnax, hurling everyone to the floor.

And Fontaine yelled *Cyclone!*

CHAPTER THREE

Ant grabbed a table leg and clung on. The giant swells and waves of the storm rocked the Aronnax so much it felt as if his arms were being torn from their sockets. The floor dipped and bucked under him like a wild horse. Fontaine had fallen to her hands and knees, hair covering her face. Before Ant could do anything to help, she slid past him, her body crumpling against Will's feet as their dad braced himself against a doorframe.

'Take the Aronnax down!' yelled Will. 'We'll be safer underwater!'

'I'm trying!' Kaiko called back. She was clinging on to the console with one hand while her finger jabbed at the submerge button. Her face was flushed. 'It's not working!'

'What the –?' Will was helping Fontaine to her feet as she brushed the hair out of her eyes. 'What's wrong? We'd normally be fifty metres under by now!'

'The ballast tanks aren't filling!' said Kaiko. 'And before you ask – no, I don't know why!'

Ant felt his body go weightless as the cyclone lifted the Aronnax and dragged it through the water at incredible speed. He saw huge waves smashing against the Plexiglas windows.

'Whooooaaa!' cried Fontaine. 'This is –'

CRRAACK!

Something smashed into the window. Ant

caught a brief glimpse of a big, dark shape, like the curved prow of a boat. The next second it was gone. All that was left was a long, jagged, forked-lightning crack in the glass.

'What was *that*?' shouted Kaiko.

'The glass –' said Will. He fought his way across the wildly pitching floor and rubbed his hand over the window. 'Seems to be holding, thank goodness!'

'But what hit us?' demanded Fontaine.

'It looked like a fishing boat,' said Ant.

'What's it doing out in the middle of a storm like this?' said Fontaine.

'Might have been the boat that sent the SOS,' said Will. 'If only this wind would drop, we could try to –'

An enormous wave smacked against the window, making the whole submarine shudder. Ant stumbled and fell. He scrambled up, looking to see if the cracked Plexiglas was still holding. It was.

So far.

'Can't you get us out of this, Mum?' begged Fontaine.

'I can't control the sub,' Kaiko said. 'The cyclone's too strong – all we can do is go with the wind.'

The cyclone redoubled its fury, seizing the Aronnax and lifting it clear of the water. For a few seconds they were rushing through the air, and then the belly of the submarine smashed back down on the turbulent sea. The Nektons staggered and collapsed in a tangled heap.

'Everyone needs to buckle up!' Will said. He reached for a lever on the wall and tugged it.

At once, ropes and webbing dropped from the ceiling.

Ant reached out to rescue his Jorange. Gripping it under one arm, he managed to wind a harness around his waist and strap himself in. Across the deck, he saw Will help Fontaine into her harness and then snap his own buckle into place. Kaiko somehow wrestled her body into a harness while clinging on to the console.

Beneath Ant's arm, Jeffrey was looking distinctly seasick. There was a miniature cyclone raging in the Jorange too.

'Don't worry, little buddy,' said Ant. He slung the Jorange on to his back. 'You'll be safe with me!'

Another thought struck him – the Circlotron! He tried to reach for it, straining at the straps of his harness.

'Ant!' warned Kaiko. 'Don't mess about. This is serious!'

'But I have to protect the Circlotron!' He reached as far as he could, his fingertips scrabbling through the air. Then his hand closed around the Circlotron and he was able to scoop it from its holder. Working quickly, he tucked it safely away in the Jorange alongside Jeffrey.

'We're going to have to ride this out and wait for the storm to drop,' said Will.

'And hope that crack in the window doesn't split open,' said Kaiko. 'Because if it does ...'

There was a pause as they all imagined the angry water rushing in.

'Oh, thanks, Mum!' said Fontaine sarcastically. 'Way to cheer everyone up!'

The wind and waves continued to batter the Aronnax as it hurtled through the storm, rising and falling and twisting like a rollercoaster. Only there was no one in charge of this rollercoaster ride, thought Ant. Except the elements.

'How long does a cyclone usually go on for?' he asked weakly.

'They've been known to last for up to a week,' Fontaine told him.

'Oh, thanks, Fontaine!' said Ant, mimicking her. 'Way to cheer everyone up!'

The next instant, there was a huge

THUNK! – as if the Aronnax had been struck from below by a giant fist. The whole submarine bucked and jumped into the air.

The Nektons were thrown upwards in their harnesses. The straps dug viciously into Ant's shoulders – he could feel angry red welts appearing beneath his wetsuit.

This is too much, Ant thought, sweat prickling in his armpits. If this was a fairground ride, he definitely wanted to get off.

There was another, smaller *thunk*.

The Aronnax came to a standstill. The wind and spray continued to rush past the windows. But they were no longer moving with the storm.

'Er ... what just happened?' said Ant.

'I think we must have run aground,' Will said. 'Hit a low-lying island.'

'So ... we're safe?' asked Fontaine.

'It all depends on what you mean by safe,' said Will, daring to unbuckle his harness. 'But at least we're not going anywhere for the time being.'

The other Nektons also unstrapped themselves. Ant took the Jorange from his back and looked in at Jeffrey. 'Are you all right, little buddy?'

Jeffrey looked sad and slightly unwell.

'I've never heard of a fish being seasick before,' Ant said. 'Don't worry, you'll get over it. Let's go and see where we are.'

Ant's legs wobbled as he walked towards the window. It felt strange that the floor wasn't moving any more. He peered out, but it was impossible to see anything much. Dark clouds rushed across the sky at frightening speed. The ground in front of them seemed to be a level expanse of black rock, but the air was so thick with spray and debris that he could only see a few metres ahead of the Aronnax.

'Shall we go and explore?' he said.

'Are you crazy?' said Will. 'In a wind like

this you'd be swept out to sea and never seen again!'

'Off you go then, Ant!' said Fontaine.

Ant made a face at his sister.

'I'll tell you what's really bugging me,' said Kaiko slowly. 'It's not the cyclone, it's the way the Aronnax is malfunctioning. We lost our satellite connection – why? That's never happened before. Then the sub wouldn't dive, which I'm guessing means a problem with the ballast tanks. Two malfunctions of completely different systems at the same time? There's got to be some reason for it – but what?'

'You're right,' said Will. 'We need to check those systems out. But we can't do much about it right now. I reckon all we can do is sit tight until the cyclone blows itself out.'

Ant stared out at the storm. They were stuck here. And what had happened to the boat that had crashed into them? It was out there ... somewhere. He shuddered. *I wouldn't want to be out there on my own.*

They gathered around a table to eat a simple supper. The storm continued to rage outside. Ant dropped some fish food into the Jorange for Jeffrey – but the fish merely looked at it and turned away with a nauseous expression.

'I don't blame you,' Ant whispered, looking sadly at his own plate of food. 'I don't have much of an appetite myself.'

'Reckon we might as well turn in,' said Will after a while. 'There's nothing more we can do today. If the wind drops tomorrow we can check out the Aronnax's systems – and try to find the boat that sent the SOS.'

'Do you think they could have survived?' asked Kaiko.

'We can only hope,' said Will.

Kaiko stood up. 'Right, kids – clean your teeth and get to bed.'

Lying on his back in his bunk, Ant closed his eyes and tried to ignore the howling wind outside. But it was impossible to sleep. He could feel the submarine rocking. How incredibly strong that cyclone must be to move a massive two-hundred-and-fifty-metre vessel like the Aronnax!

He opened his eyes. Through the window a new moon was visible, like a fingernail paring, with scraps of black cloud racing past it. Did that have anything to do with the violence of the cyclone, he wondered? The moon influenced the tides, he knew that. He sat up and reached for his tablet. Maybe he could find out a little more about cyclones and whether a new moon affected them.

Ant soon found what he was looking for. It was true: a scientific study had found that cyclones happened more frequently when there was a new moon, and they were usually fiercer too. But nobody was quite sure why ...

A shadow appeared in the gap of light beneath his bedroom door.

'Ant,' came his father's deep voice from the hallway. 'Put the device away, please. Time to sleep.'

Ant sighed. It was like his dad could see through walls!

He put the tablet down and closed his eyes. Whatever mysteries lay beyond the walls of the Aronnax ... for now, they'd have to wait.

CHAPTER FOUR

'Oh, look, it's the walking dead,' said Fontaine as Ant shuffled into the galley area, carrying his tablet under his arm. He'd been woken by sunlight streaming through the porthole of his cabin. The storm had passed.

The rest of the Nektons sat with cereal bowls in front of them, and Will reached to pour himself a second cup of coffee.

'Oh, leave him alone,' said Kaiko. 'He needs

his beauty sleep, don't you, Ant?'

'It would take more than a night's sleep to make him beautiful,' said Fontaine.

'All right, enough,' said Will. 'Let's plan our day. First, we need to try and track down the boat that sent the SOS. And hope we're not too late to help.'

'The distress signal hasn't been repeated,' Kaiko said. 'It might not be in the area any more.'

Ant hoped that didn't mean the boat had sunk.

'Do you think they could have run aground, like us?' asked Fontaine.

'It's possible,' Will said. 'This is a good-sized island. I've looked it up on the chart.'

'Let's go out and search!' said Ant.

'I think that's a very good plan,' Will said. 'You and Fontaine go. The island's inhabited – you can ask if anyone has seen anything. Meanwhile, your mother and I can inspect the damage we've suffered.'

'Yes!' Kaiko clapped her hands. 'I need to get down to work. First thing to sort out are those ballast tanks. A submarine that won't submerge – something's wrong there!' She slid open a cupboard door, took out a tool belt and attached it around her waist.

'And I'll need to replace that cracked window,' Will said. 'That'll take most of the morning.'

'Come on then, Fontaine!' Ant leaped to his feet and slung on his Jorange, with the Circlotron still slotted inside next to Jeffrey. 'Let's go exploring!'

'Hold on,' Fontaine said, with her hands on her hips. 'You're seriously going to take that fish? And the Circlotron? The priority is finding the boat that needs help, not your toys.'

'I'm not leaving Jeffrey on his own. Mum and Dad are going to be busy working – what if someone sneaked in and stole him?'

'I don't think that's very likely, Ant,' said Kaiko.

'They'd have to be a pretty dumb thief,' commented Fontaine.

In the Jorange, Jeffrey looked directly at Fontaine.

'That's not funny!' Ant said. 'You've offended Jeffrey. I can tell by his face that he's really upset.'

'Yeah, because fish have such expressive faces, don't they?' said Fontaine.

'Let him take his pet if he likes,' said Will.

'And the Circlotron?' Fontaine peered at the small globe with the Lemurian etchings. 'I mean, why? It's asking for trouble. Just like when you took it on to the Dark Orca.'

'Yeah, but we definitely shouldn't leave the Circlotron unprotected while Mum and Dad are busy. Any thief would want this!'

'Just stop bickering, you two, and get out there!' Kaiko touched a pad on the instrument panel and the Aronnax doors silently slid open. Sunlight flooded in.

'So, we'll ask everyone we meet if they've seen the fishing boat,' said Ant as they walked through the doors. 'And while we're at it we could ask if they know who King Batu is!'

'You're obsessed!' said Fontaine. 'It's more important we find that boat that needed help.'

They stepped out into the fresh air. The breeze was warm on Ant's cheeks. Beneath their feet was dark, volcanic rock, with little clumps of coarse, springy grass still lying flat after the storm. Broken tree branches and palm fronds were strewn around.

They began to walk up a gentle hill, waving goodbye to the Aronnax. Ant saw that it had suffered some damage in the storm; as well as the jagged crack in the window there were scratches all along its sides and it was smeared with sand, mud and seaweed. Even though he lived in the world's oceans, it was still amazing

to him – and a bit terrifying – to think how much power the water could yield.

The hill grew steeper. Ant spotted a lizard dart away across a rock, and he began to pant in the heat of the sun. Eventually they arrived at the top of the hill and his gaze scanned the coastline. The island was like nothing Ant had ever seen before. In the far distance, he could see a cluster of buildings. At the heart of the island was a valley, verdant and lush. In stark contrast, the beach was an expanse of pure white sand skirting the glittering sea.

'It's like looking at two totally different terrains rolled into one,' he said. But Fontaine wasn't listening – she'd been searching the water and the horizon for any sign of a boat, and now she was staring hard at a shape on the beach.

A figure was crouched at the water's edge.

'Let's go and talk to him,' said Fontaine.

As Ant and Fontaine approached, the figure

stood up and faced them. He was tall, with gold-rimmed spectacles and a black moustache. He was holding a glass beaker full of seawater, and on the sand beside him was an open case full of scientific instruments. He stared with narrowed eyes at Ant and Fontaine, as though the siblings were a pair of interesting specimens.

'Hello! Where did you spring from?' he asked.

'From our submarine. We were washed up here in the storm,' Fontaine said, cheerfully pointing over the hill. 'I'm Fontaine Nekton. And this is Ant.'

'My name's actually Antaeus,' said Ant, a bit annoyed that his sister had got in first with the introductions. 'But everyone calls me Ant.'

The scientist raised his eyebrows. 'You didn't hear the cyclone warning, then?'

That was the second time someone had mentioned a failed warning – first Kaiko, and now this scientist. Ant felt a prickle of unease. It was odd that the WOA hadn't been able to get any message through to them.

'Our satellite system went down,' Ant explained. 'We've been following a route along the celestial equator.'

'Along the celestial equator?' the man echoed.

Fontaine flashed Ant a warning look, but he was already scrabbling to pull the Circlotron out of his Jorange.

'Using this!' He proudly held out the small orb.

'Ah. So you're stargazers,' said the man, eyeing the globe. He took a step back, as though scared to touch it, and Ant began to think that maybe he shouldn't have brought it out. It had been hidden beneath the ocean for thousands of years – should he be showing it to total strangers? He eased it back into the floating lid of the Jorange.

'Not exactly stargazers,' said Fontaine, frowning at Ant. 'Our submarine is state-of-the-art. The Aronnax. We usually steer using satellite technology, but we had a few problems in the storm. Our mum and dad are repairing it right now.'

'You're lucky it's repairable. I haven't seen many cyclones as bad as that one.'

'I expect the new moon made it worse,' Ant said knowledgeably.

Fontaine rolled her eyes, but the scientist looked at Ant with respect. 'You're probably right. My name is Dr Fesuzia, by the way. The storm did a lot of damage here too – it's going to take a long time to clear it up.' He pointed down the beach, where a crowd of people were at work, picking up pieces of wreckage. 'It destroyed half our village.'

Dr Fesuzia put a stopper in the top of his beaker and stowed it away in his case of instruments. 'Well, nice talking to you. I must take this back to my lab to analyse.'

Ant couldn't suppress his curiosity. If there were scientific investigations happening, he wanted to be in on them. 'Can we help? I'm a bit of a scientist myself, you know. Well, an inventor. I invented the Jorange!' He pointed proudly at his backpack with Jeffrey swimming around in his tank of water.

Dr Fesuzia grinned. 'Impressive.'

'So, what is it you're analysing?' asked Fontaine. The three of them started to walk along the shore towards the village.

'Well, when a cyclone churns up the waves to that extent, it tends to deplete the oxygen levels, and makes the water more saline –'

'He means salty,' Fontaine told Ant.

'Well, duh-ur,' Ant said. 'I did know that, actually!'

'And salinity wouldn't be great news for the king,' Dr Fesuzia finished.

'The king?' Ant asked in excitement. There was actual royalty living on the island? Maybe I could meet the king, he thought. He began to indulge in a fantasy where the king was so impressed with his invention that he knighted him. Or better still, knighted Jeffrey. Sir Jeffrey of the Jorange ...

There was a shout from further down the beach. A figure was running towards them, kicking up sand.

'Dr Fesuzia! Dr Fesuzia!' the woman cried, stumbling to a halt in front of them. She rested her hands on her thighs as she drew ragged breaths.

Dr Fesuzia placed a hand on her shoulder. 'What is it? What's happened?'

The villager pointed back down the beach. 'Someone's been washed up,' she panted. 'She's alive, but – she needs your help!'

CHAPTER FIVE

Dr Fesuzia broke into a run, following the woman along the shore. Ant and Fontaine looked at each other, nodded and ran after them.

They caught up just as Dr Fesuzia reached a group of villagers gathered on the shoreline. The crowd parted and Ant saw that a fishing boat had been washed up. Its name, 'The Outcast', was written in curling script on

the stern. It was large, with armoured metal plates along its sides and a sharp, jutting prow. It immediately reminded Ant of the object that had crashed into the Aronnax and cracked their window. Could it be the same vessel?

A young woman was lying on her back, eyes closed, in the bottom of the boat. She was wearing a strange wetsuit, slick and grey and slightly furry, like the pelt of a seal.

Dr Fesuzia leaned over the side of the vessel. 'Hello? Can you hear me?'

The woman's eyes opened. She looked startled. With an effort she hauled herself to her feet. She rested her weight against a large wooden box with an open lid. It was full of tools: spanners, wrenches, soldering irons.

'Are you all right?' asked the doctor.

She passed a hand across her forehead. 'I must have passed out.'

'The king!' muttered one of the villagers.

'Yes, it must be the work of the king,' said another.

'The king, the king!' The murmured words ran through the crowd like an electric current.

Ant and Fontaine exchanged a puzzled look. How could the king possibly have been responsible for the young woman fainting in her boat?

'I'd better check you over,' said Dr Fesuzia. He vaulted lightly into the boat. 'Let me see if there are any puncture wounds.' He took out a magnifying glass from his case and examined the woman's wetsuit, looking with particular care at the feet. 'I just need to check you haven't sustained any injuries from poisoned barbs. Don't worry, I have antidotes with me if necessary ...'

'Why would he think she's been poisoned?' Ant whispered.

Fontaine shrugged, her face blank.

But the doctor appeared to be satisfied

with his examination. 'You're fine,' he told the woman. 'Just a bit shaken up. That was quite a storm last night, eh? Here, give me your arm and I'll help you out. People – can you stand back?'

The crowd backed away, and with Dr Fesuzia's help the young woman clambered out of the boat. She stood for a moment on the sand. Then her knees buckled, and before the doctor could catch her she slumped to the ground. The villagers muttered among themselves.

'All right, don't try to get up just yet,' he said. 'Get your strength back. Tell me – who are you?'

'My name is Edwina,' the woman said faintly. 'I was out on a mission.' Her face suddenly creased in pain and they had to wait for her to continue her story. After a moment or two, she wiped a hand across her face. 'But I was caught up in the cyclone. My boat ... hit something.'

Her gaze came to rest on Ant's face and he felt himself flush – then her eyes rolled back in her head and she gave a moan.

So it was her who hit us! Ant thought. He opened his mouth to speak, but ...

'She certainly likes a drama,' Fontaine whispered out of the side of her mouth.

Dr Fesuzia was bent over the woman, asking her more questions as he gently rubbed her back. 'What was your mission?'

'Help me up, please.' She reached out a trembling hand and the doctor helped her to her feet. Some instinct made Ant shrink back behind a villager, pulling Fontaine with him. He hadn't liked it when her gaze had caught his.

'I have an urgent message to deliver from the WOA,' she said in a formal voice, looking around. 'It's for the crew of a vessel called the Aronnax.' A frown creased her brow. So she hadn't recognised Ant as a Nekton – why did that make him feel better? 'Apparently, they can't be reached by satellite communication. Has anyone here seen or heard anything of the Aronnax?'

She looked from face to face.

'Why are we hiding?' Fontaine whispered to Ant, though she seemed willing to follow his lead.

Ant shook his head. 'I don't know. I just have a bad feeling about this.'

'Yes, indeed,' said Dr Fesuzia. He peered into the crowd. 'Two of their crew are here ... somewhere.' He frowned. 'Or they were a minute ago. Has anyone seen ... ?'

Ant felt a sudden dig in his back and he was shoved forward by a villager. Fontaine quickly stepped up beside him and he felt a rush of gratitude. She wouldn't let him face this alone.

Dr Fesuzia's face brightened. 'Ah, here they are!' He gestured for them to move closer. 'These are our new friends from the Aronnax.

Their sub has run aground on the other side of the island. Strange coincidence!'

Edwina gazed at Ant and Fontaine with a bright, friendly face. If she'd figured they'd been hiding from her, she didn't let it show. 'How lucky to meet you here! I have orders from Commander Pyrosome.'

'Oh yes?' said Fontaine – Ant could tell she shared his suspicions. What was it about Edwina that made them so uneasy?

'The commander wants a scientific investigation of a device you're in possession of. A small metal orb. It probably doesn't look like much to you, but we need to examine it.'

Ant felt his heartbeat suddenly begin to race. If he was suspicious before, now his senses were on high alert. How did this woman know about the Circlotron? Likewise Commander Pyrosome? He could feel its weight in the Jorange hanging on his back.

'I told you to leave it on the Aronnax!' Fontaine hissed.

'What's that? You have it with you?' Edwina's expression became sharp and watchful. 'Show it to me.' She moved towards Ant, her hand held out, fingers trembling with anticipation.

This doesn't feel right. Not right at all, Ant thought, and wished with every cell in his body to be back on the Aronnax. Whose idea had it been to bring it anyway? *Oh yeah. Mine*.

He backed away. 'It's ours – you can't have it!' Why was he suddenly talking like a sulky child? Fontaine was staring at him.

'Oh yes I can, and I will!' Edwina stepped closer.

The crowd shifted from foot to foot and Dr Fesuzia's face was creased with anxiety.

'Excuse me,' the doctor said, stepping between Edwina and the Nektons. 'You do have authorisation, don't you?'

'Authorisation?' Edwina's face cleared, turning innocent again. 'Oh, of course, yes, I have authorisation. Excellent authorisation from the very highest level.' She patted the pockets of her wetsuit, as though looking for something. 'Let me see. Now, where is that ... ?'

Before she'd finished speaking, she darted around Dr Fesuzia and threw herself at Ant, taking them all by surprise. She ripped at the straps of the Jorange, dragging it from his shoulders.

'Hey, stop that!' Ant shouted, struggling to hold on to the Jorange as Fontaine tried to push Edwina away.

But Edwina was too quick and too strong. With one hand she gave Fontaine a shove that sent her reeling, while with the other she twisted the Jorange from Ant's grasp.

'So kind of you to cooperate! I'll tell Commander Pyrosome about your helpful attitude!'

She slung the Jorange over one shoulder and leaped back into her boat. The whole fainting fit – it had been one big act. There was no doubting her energy and strength now.

'Stop her!' shouted Ant.

Dr Fesuzia and the villagers raced towards the boat – but it was too late.

Edwina reached for something in the interior and everyone gasped as a gleaming metal shell rose and snapped shut over the boat. Dr Fesuzia had to snatch his hand back to avoid losing his fingers.

Edwina had disappeared beneath the silver carapace.

The boat's engines roared into life. With a churning of sand and surf it moved into the shallows. Frantically, Ant ran after it, up to his knees in the water. He beat on the metal shell with his fists. 'My Circlotron! Jeffrey! Give them back!'

The boat moved away, picking up speed.

Ant tripped and fell in the surf, salt water blinding him.

The Outcast suddenly accelerated like a torpedo. It shot away, leaving behind a white creamy wake.

By the time Ant climbed back on his feet it was a dot on the horizon.

His hands hung helplessly by his sides. His Jorange was gone.

His Circlotron was gone.

And Jeffrey was gone.

CHAPTER SIX

There was a stunned silence.

'I'm sorry,' said Dr Fesuzia. 'I had no idea –'

'It's not your fault,' said Ant, wading back on to the beach. His mind was still reeling. He looked at Fontaine. 'I've lost the Circlotron. And even worse, she's got Jeffrey. I'll never see them again!'

'Yes, you will,' said Fontaine, laying a hand on his shoulder. 'We'll chase Edwina to the ends of the Earth and somehow we'll –'

'But how?' said Ant despairingly.

There was a sudden gasp from the woman who'd raced to find Dr Fesuzia. She was pointing to the ocean with a trembling hand.

They all followed the line of her finger.

'What is that?' said Dr Fesuzia.

The massive form of the Aronnax – a quarter kilometre long – had come into view in front of the bay. Ant felt a rush of pride to see the titanium hull glittering in the sunshine. It cruised towards them and stopped a little way out, sending waves rolling over the sand and wetting the feet of the villagers.

'That's the Aronnax,' said Fontaine.

'That's home.' Ant grinned.

Dr Fesuzia gave a low whistle. 'Impressive.'

The turret at the top of the submarine opened and the figure of Will appeared, waving. 'We're all fixed up!' he called.

Ant's spurt of pride disappeared as quickly as it had arrived. Now he'd have to tell his parents what had happened.

'Come on.' Without stopping to say goodbye, he ran into the surf, closely followed by Fontaine. They swam the last few metres and climbed up the steel ladder their father had lowered.

'Goodbye!' called Dr Fesuzia, waving after them. 'And good luck!'

Ant barely paused to shout back, 'Thanks!'

He and Fontaine scrambled on board and went through the door on the top deck. The elevator whisked them down to the bridge.

Kaiko glanced up from the control deck. The moment she saw Ant's stricken face, her eyes widened with concern.

'Are you OK, Ant?'

'Jorange gone – and the Circlotron – she was in a boat and she had a wetsuit like a seal – and she's got Jeffrey – and the lid closed and –'

'Hey, slow down!' Will guided Ant to a seat.

Fontaine took up the story as Ant collapsed on to the chair, explaining what had happened. 'So, the Jorange, the Circlotron – they're gone,' she finished. 'One minute they were there, the next ...' She snapped her fingers. 'Edwina snatched them.'

Ant could hardly bring himself to look at his family. He'd let them down – badly.

'Well,' said Will, after a long pause. He looked at Kaiko and she gave him a discreet nod. 'We'll soon pick up this Edwina on the sonar. Her boat may be fast but I very much doubt it's as fast as the Aronnax.'

He went over to the monitor and set the sonar scanner for a long-range sweep. A green circle appeared on the screen with a line sweeping around it. Halfway around the circuit, it gave a *ping* and a black dot appeared at the edge of the screen as the line passed through it.

'Got her!' said Will. 'Kaiko?'

'I'm on it,' said Kaiko. She pressed the submerge button. 'Luckily, I managed to fix the ballast tanks. Something very strange happened there, I think they might have been tampered with ...' She frowned and shook her head. 'Anyway, no time to worry about that now.'

As she pressed the submerge button, the island disappeared from view and the sub smoothly dived below the surface. Kaiko pulled the throttle towards her. Ant felt the power surge as the mighty submarine accelerated through the glassy green water.

He watched the needle on the speedometer swing swiftly round to the Aronnax's top speed: fifty knots. He desperately hoped they would be able to rescue the two things most precious to him in all the world. 'We will catch her, won't we?' he asked his parents.

'Oh yes. There's no way she can outrun us,' his mother assured him.

'And when we catch up with her she'll have some questions to answer,' Will said grimly. 'This is all mighty strange. Who is she, and how did she know about the Circlotron?'

'She said she worked for the WOA,' said Fontaine. 'To be fair, she did know our satellite link was down.'

'I've fixed the satellite link,' said Kaiko. 'So we can check that out right now!'

She keyed in the code on the video link to connect to the WOA. A moment later, the screen filled with the unsmiling face of Commander Pyrosome. Her hair was cropped short like a soldier's and she wore the dark blue uniform of the Worldwide Oceanic Authority. Ant had never seen her out of uniform; he had a theory that she slept in it.

'Yes?' snapped Commander Pyrosome.

'Hello, Commander, how are you?' Kaiko

began with exaggerated politeness. Ant bit his lip to stop himself from smiling. 'We have a query for you. Do you employ someone called Edwina? She has a boat called the ... what's it called, kids?'

'The Outcast,' said Fontaine.

'The Worldwide Oceanic Authority is a huge organisation, as I'm sure you are aware,' said Commander Pyrosome in her precise, clipped tones. 'Directly or indirectly, we employ over twenty thousand people. One of them might be called Edwina, I really couldn't say. Now I'm afraid I'm rather busy, so if you'll excuse me –'

'Wait!' said Will. 'Commander, we're asking you for help.' Did Ant see the face up on the screen soften ever so slightly?

'Go on,' she said after a moment.

'OK.' Will took a deep breath and threw Kaiko a glance that said, 'I'll take it from here'. 'Did you recently inform an agent that the

Aronnax's satellite link was down? And send her on a mission to get the Circlotron from us?'

'No, I didn't,' said Commander Pyrosome. She looked perplexed. 'Who is this person? I've never heard of a Circlotron. What's going on?'

'Hey, look!' said Ant, pointing at the sonar. The black dot was almost at the centre of the screen now, and the *pings* were virtually continuous.

'I'm afraid we're rather busy, Commander, so if you'll excuse us –' said Kaiko, and zapped off the link before she could respond.

'And now for a word with the mysterious Edwina!' said Will.

'I'll take us up,' said Kaiko.

The Aronnax rose and daylight spilt in through the windows once more. Ant saw the Outcast, no more than a stone's throw away. It was still travelling, leaving a wake behind it – but they were getting nearer with every second.

'What is that? It looks like a giant mollusc shell,' Will said.

'Some sort of ... metal lid that covers her boat. It nearly took off the doctor's hand when it snapped shut,' Ant said.

'All right, let's see if she can hear through that thing.' Will flipped on the electronic address system and spoke into the microphone. 'Ahoy there! You cannot escape. Give yourself up and return what you have stolen. Repeat, give yourself up!'

The titanium shell covering the Outcast slid back to reveal Edwina standing in the boat. Kaiko gasped. There was no denying it, the other woman looked impressive in her strange wetsuit, her short dark hair escaping from the diving mask that was pushed back on her head. The Jorange was on her back, and as she turned slightly Ant caught a flash of purple and gold. So Jeffrey was still there, unharmed.

Thank goodness, he thought. *She's going to come quietly* ...

But he was wrong. Edwina scrambled to the back of the boat and sat on the side. There was a dazzling flash of silver in the sunlight.

'Crazy outfit!' said Fontaine.

The whole of Edwina's bottom half was covered in some sort of metallic layer. It looked like liquid silver – or armour – or ...

'It's like a seal's tail,' Kaiko murmured. They stared as if hypnotised as the tips of Edwina's tail began to rotate round and round, so fast it became a blur. The next moment, she slipped into the water and disappeared from view. The Outcast bobbed, abandoned on the ocean.

Edwina had gone.

'What the –?' said Will, turning to stare at the other Nektons. 'What was that?'

Ant felt stunned, unable to reply.

'That's no ordinary woman,' Kaiko said, wandering over to rest her hands against the

window. Her breath misted on the Plexiglas. 'She's ...'

'She's a selkie!' Ant finished for her. He'd read about the mythical creatures – humans on land, seals in the water. He'd never in his life imagined he'd see one with his very own eyes.

'I didn't expect that,' said Will, scratching his head.

Kaiko shook herself, as though coming out of a trance. Then she strode back to the control deck and cut the Aronnax's engines.

'Not easy to chase her in the sub,' Kaiko said. 'We're not manoeuvrable enough.'

'And in that selkie suit she's too small to show up on the sonar,' Will said. 'We wouldn't be able to distinguish her from a big fish or a dolphin.'

'We could go after her in the Knights!' said Fontaine. 'Ant?'

But Ant was already racing past her to the Moon Pool.

CHAPTER SEVEN

Ant climbed into the Shadow Knight. It was the quickest of the Aronnax's exploration suits. The exterior was light grey, but it turned darker when in stealth mode, giving him a good chance of catching up with Edwina unobserved.

Without waiting for Fontaine, Ant plunged into the Moon Pool and swam out from under the Aronnax. He fired up the jets of the

Shadow Knight and zoomed through the water, following the direction Edwina had taken. Her velvety wetsuit looked like it could zip through the water like a seal, but it wouldn't be as fast as his Shadow Knight – he hoped.

The ocean floor sped below him, fronds swaying in his slipstream as he darted around rocks and skirted rainbow-coloured shoals of fish. He switched on the display screen on the inside of the cockpit, which was positioned so he could view it simply by raising his eyes. The hidden screen showed a magnified display of his surroundings, which allowed him to see further ahead – like having an onboard telescope. His heartbeat quickened as he glimpsed the outline of Edwina swimming ahead of him in the distance.

She didn't know he was behind her – yet.

If I can just get closer before she looks round.

Darting between rocks, he approached

carefully. He no longer needed his display screen – he was close enough to make out the individual metal scales on her tail. The fin whirred in a blur, sending up columns of bubbles. He spotted the Jorange on her back, with the Circlotron inside. Jeffrey was swimming in tight, anxious circles inside his tank. Ant had to rescue him – and the Circlotron! But how?

'What's happening down there?' came a familiar voice. Will was sending a message from the Aronnax.

'I've found Edwina,' Ant whispered back. He didn't know why he was whispering, but it wouldn't surprise him if Edwina had a way of intercepting their radio messages. 'I'm going to try and grab the Jorange from her.'

'You should have waited for your sister, Ant.'

'It's too late for that now,' he messaged back.

'OK, she's not far behind you. Good luck.'

Will's voice crackled. Luck – Ant was going to need a lot of that. He hadn't actually planned what his next move was going to be. *Maybe if I take Edwina by surprise I can pull the Jorange off before she knows what's happening*, he thought. *Just a little bit closer ...*

Ant swam out from behind a rock, careful to avoid any sudden, jerky movements. He hovered in the water just behind Edwina. Jeffrey spotted him and stared pleadingly through the glass of the Jorange, his mouth opening and closing as if saying, 'Help!'

'Don't worry, Jeffrey, I'll save you,' Ant muttered under his breath. He extended the Knight's arms to grab the straps of the Jorange. Slowly, slowly ...

No! A shaft of sunlight pierced the water and Ant's shadow fell across Edwina. She realised she was being pursued, glanced round and with a flip of her metallic tail shot downwards. Desperately, Ant lunged to grab the Jorange, but the Knight's pincers closed around empty water. He was too late.

Twisting and turning like an eel, Edwina made for a nearby coral forest. Silvery fish darted in and out of glowing fronds of green, red, yellow, orange, turquoise and purple. The beautiful delicate forest took his breath away, but he had no time to admire the view. He glanced round, looking for any sign of Fontaine but ... *I can't wait! I have to go after Edwina.*

'I'm going into a coral forest,' he messaged. 'We're south-west of the sub!' Then, without waiting for an answer, he plunged into the coral.

He looked around wildly. There! He could just make out the shape of Edwina, but she was zigzagging in and out of the coral and it was hard to keep track of her. As he moved deeper into the forest, the water filled with silt and sediment and it became more and more difficult to see anything. He realised that the

coral must have been damaged by the cyclone, and Edwina was taking full advantage of the camouflage.

Ant's shoulders slumped inside his Knight. He had completely lost sight of her. There was no point zooming along in the wrong direction. He came to a stop beside an underwater mountain that rose up beside the coral reef. The mountain towered steeply over him, rising all the way to the surface. Ant stared around to see if he could catch a glimpse of Edwina. Maybe she'd dodged round the other side?

He would get a better view if he rose closer to the surface, he decided, away from the clouds of coral dust. Then he might be able to spot Edwina from above. The suit powered him up towards the summit of the mountain. Near the ocean surface it flattened out to form a shelf that was littered with large flat mottled stones.

Ant began to swim slowly around, scanning the depths below him, pushing against the stones to propel himself along.

Suddenly, he heard a clunk and felt a sharp blow against the armoured pincer of his Knight – a blow strong enough to push him back through the water. What the –?

He glanced back.

'It can't be,' he whispered.

One of the stones was moving slowly towards him. Not rolling in the tide or sliding across the shelf but ... swimming! Those were fins, moving through the water as a hinged jaw gradually opened and closed. A pair of bulging eyes snapped open. The stone wasn't a stone. His mind scrolled through all the creatures he'd seen in the ocean. An image clicked into place.

He radioed through to the Aronnax. 'There's a giant stonefish down here!' he gasped.

'Wow! How big?' came Will's voice.

Ant did some rapid calculations, his eyes scanning the creature. 'Giant – at least two metres.' Thank goodness for his armoured suit! If he'd put an unprotected hand or foot on it, it would have stabbed a poisoned barb into him for sure. And that would not have been fun.

He heard a crackling sound down the line. 'The stonefish is the most venomous fish in all the oceans, Ant!' He could hear the tension in his mother's voice. 'Please – be careful.'

'Don't worry, Mum,' he reassured her. She'd kill me if I died from a stonefish jab, he thought, joking grimly to himself.

He stared as the stonefish lazily moved through the water. It was enormous. And ugly enough to win prizes. Its skin was knobbly and mottled grey and brown like the surrounding rocks. It had bulbous black eyes and a crumpled, downturned mouth that made it look like a grumpy old man.

Ant wondered how old it must be to have grown to such a size. There was something stately, almost regal about its progress. Did the people on the island know about this creature, he wondered?

Then something seemed to click in his mind. Of course they knew! He remembered Dr Fesuzia checking Edwina for poisoned barbs, and saying that the king wouldn't like it if the salinity of the water increased. This monstrous old stonefish was what they called the king!

The stonefish continued to swim, its fins flapping gently but moving with surprising speed, and Ant followed a little way behind. He was fascinated by the strange creature – so big, so ugly, so dangerous, yet so oddly graceful.

And then, a little way ahead, he spied Edwina. She had her back to him and was slowly moving through the shallows. She must have thought she'd escaped and was working out her next move. The Jorange was still strapped to her back and Ant could see the tiny purple and gold shape of Jeffrey.

The stonefish seemed to spot Edwina too. It accelerated and started to swim purposefully towards her, clearly furious at not one but two trespassers in its underwater realm.

'Edwina!' shouted Ant through his radio mic, waving his arms to attract her attention. So much for going undercover. Edwina might be his enemy but he couldn't let her get stung by a giant stonefish. 'Look out!'

Startled, Edwina turned. The stonefish was almost on her.

She jackknifed and tried to dart past it to safety. But the stonefish lunged at her and caught the strap of the Jorange in its jaws. There was a brief struggle. Edwina's eyes

bulged in panic. Then, in desperation, she shrugged off the other strap and swam away, her tail corkscrewing like crazy. She vanished into a forest of seagrass some way off – leaving the stonefish with the Jorange dangling from its mouth. Jeffrey was swimming around in panicked circles.

'Good boy!' said Ant, approaching slowly. He held out a pincer. 'Good king! Let's have it, then.'

The stonefish gave him a defiant stare as it slowly backed away. *Hmm, this isn't going to work.* The fish executed a sudden turn and disappeared with its prize into a fissure between two rocks. The gap was too narrow for the Shadow Knight to follow.

And meanwhile, Edwina was hiding out in the forest of seagrass.

I could use some help right now, Ant thought.

'Next time,' came an annoyed voice, 'I

suggest you wait for me.'

Ant whirled round to see the White Knight drawing up beside him. 'Fontaine!' he cried.

Ant Nekton had never been so glad to see his sister.

CHAPTER EIGHT

What are you, crazy?' Fontaine demanded. 'Rushing off on your own without waiting for me – anything could have happened!'

'Plenty of stuff did happen,' Ant replied. 'I found Edwina!'

'Where is she, then?'

'In there.' Ant pointed to the forest of seagrass. 'I lost her again.'

Fontaine quickly inspected Ant's Knight.

'And where is the Jorange?'

Ant bit his lip. 'In there.' He pointed to the fissure. 'A stonefish has got it.'

'Well, you have done well,' said Fontaine, floating beside him. 'So, now what?'

'We need to find Edwina. But we also need to rescue Jeffrey before that fish eats him!'

'Mum? Dad?' Fontaine spoke into her radio mic. 'We're kind of in a situation here.'

'What sort of situation?' came Will's voice.

'We know where Edwina is – sort of. And we know where the Jorange with the Circlotron is – sort of. So ...'

Ant joined in the conversation. 'Dad? The stonefish has stolen the Jorange!'

'OK, now you really need to be careful!' came Kaiko's voice. 'The poison from even a small stonefish can be deadly, and what did you say this one was? Over two metres long!'

'Don't worry, Mum, we won't take any risks. It really is a beauty though – you should see it! I'm pretty sure it's what the islanders were calling "the king". And it's got Jeffrey and the Circlotron in a crevice in the side of an underwater mountain!'

'That's ... interesting,' Will said slowly. 'A mountain, you say? And the fish is called ... the king?' The sound of Will snapping his fingers was clearly audible over the radio. 'Listen, the Indonesian word for "stone" is *batu.* King Batu – remember? That's what the riddle means – the Child of the Mountain is the stonefish!'

'That definitely means we're on the right track!' Ant said.

'Yeah, OK, but what do we do right now?' said Fontaine.

'The priority is to get the Circlotron back,' said Kaiko.

'And Jeffrey!' Ant chipped in.

'Yes, and Jeffrey. Do that and return to the Aronnax,' Will said.

'Don't approach Edwina,' Kaiko said. 'She could be dangerous!'

'Yeah, like a stonefish isn't,' said Fontaine sarcastically.

'Stay safe, kids,' their father said. 'And keep us posted, OK?'

'OK.' Fontaine turned to Ant. 'All right, so how do we get it out of there?'

'I reckon it's hungry,' Ant said. 'That's why it took Jeffrey. It can't get at him, but if it breaks the glass ... !' He felt his heart flutter with anxiety. No way could he let his best friend in the whole world be swallowed up in that stonefish's grumpy mouth!

'We have to tempt the fish out,' said Fontaine, talking slowly as a plan formed in her mind. A cloud of shrimp swam past, their tiny legs scrabbling as she watched them plunge into a forest of seagrass. 'Stonefish eat crustaceans, right?'

'Do they?'

'Sure they do.' Her face shone with excitement as her eyes snapped back to Ant. 'And over there is a massive great forest of seagrass – where those shrimp hang out.'

'That's where Edwina's hanging out too,' Ant reminded her.

But Fontaine took no notice. She launched her Knight towards the seagrass and tore up a great clump of it with the robotic arms. Then she swam back to the stonefish's lair and shook the seagrass through the water, making the strands dip and sway. 'Dinner-time!' she cried. Instantly a crowd of translucent shrimp tumbled out and drifted in the water in front of the fissure.

Ant thought he saw a slight movement in the darkness – and the next moment, the stonefish cautiously emerged. The strap of the Jorange was still gripped in its jaws. Jeffrey was swimming around inside, his eyes popping with anxiety.

'Whoa!' said Fontaine. 'You weren't joking, were you? That is one massive stonefish. Don't get too near it, Ant – if that stung you, you'd die in horrible, terrible agony.'

'Yeah, thanks for the heads-up.'

'Come on, King Stoney!' said Fontaine. She shook the seagrass again and more shrimp floated out. 'Come and get this lovely shrimp buffet, yum yum yum!'

The stonefish's eyes widened. It eased forward, raising a cloud of sand. Its jaws opened – and the Jorange drifted free.

Ant sprang forward and grabbed it, cradling it in the robotic arms of the Knight. 'Jeffrey, I'll never let you go again!'

Jeffrey swam around, wagging his tail fin.

But Ant noticed something else.

'Fontaine,' he called, 'I think the Circlotron has switched on somehow.'

'I'm kind of busy right now, Ant,' she replied.

The stonefish was now hungrily hoovering

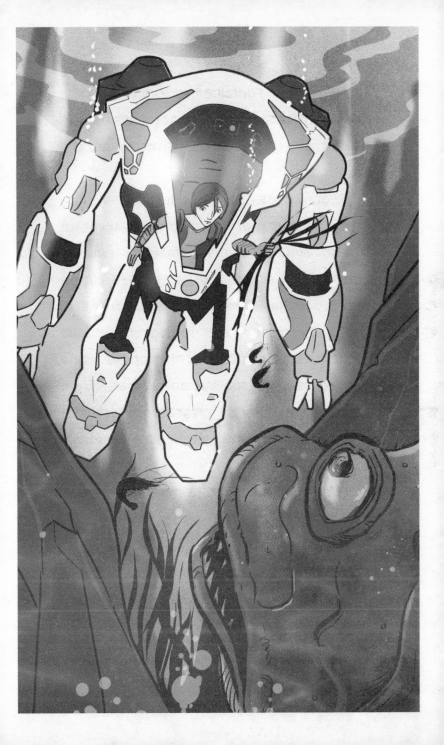

up the shrimp. Fontaine had to give it a wide berth as she swam round to Ant's side to look. 'Hey, what's this?' she said, pointing into the cave.

Engraved on the rocks just outside the stonefish's lair was a symbol – an image of a long, sinuous serpent, its body twisting and turning and its jaws wide open with a forked tongue protruding. Ant frowned, staring at the piled-up rocks of the stonefish's lair. He felt his skin prickle as he noticed how the rocks were piled neatly on top of each other to create a perfect arch that had defied centuries of tides to remain standing.

'That's no normal lair,' he murmured. 'That's human built.'

'Or Lemurian built,' added his sister. 'The carving of the snake, does it remind you of anything?' The style of it recalled mystic etchings Ant had seen on ...

'The Circlotron!' the two of them said together. Almost at the same moment, the Circlotron whirred further into life inside the Jorange. Ant's backpack was still hanging from the arm of his Knight and he felt the vibrations of its energy travel down the arm. The Circlotron shot a beam of light through the murky ocean, lighting up the etching of the snake.

This was just what had happened beside the dragon's cave, when Ant had spotted the etching of the child and the mountain. Almost at the same time, the Circlotron had juddered into life, a matching image glowing on its rim. There was no doubt about it – Ant's Circlotron was guiding him along a route, lighting up to let him know each time he'd found the next clue.

'I don't think it's a coincidence that we've found this lair,' Ant said. He looked nervously around to see if anyone else might have spotted the beam of light – someone like Edwina.

Will's voice came through on the radio. 'Any luck?' Ant and Fontaine shared a glance – where to begin?

'Yes, we've got the Circlotron,' reported Fontaine.

'And Jeffrey!' said Ant.

'Oh, yeah, and the fish.' Fontaine rolled her eyes.

'See, Jeffrey, I told you she cared,' Ant said, and his sister grinned.

'Good work,' Will said. 'OK, you two. I want you to come straight back.'

'And so do I!' came Kaiko's voice. 'Quickly.'

Ant figured they could fill their parents in on everything else once they were back on board.

'Race you back to the Aronnax, Ant!' Fontaine said, and zoomed away.

Ant started to follow her, but then slowed down to look back at the seagrass forest.

Edwina was still in there ... somewhere. Why had she been so determined to steal the Circlotron? And how did she even know about it? It was a mystery. And mysteries were there to be solved.

He spoke into his radio mic. 'Fontaine? While we're here, it seems a shame not to track Edwina down, find out what this is all about. Why does she want the Circlotron? And how does she know about it?'

'What? Ant, no!'

It was now or never. 'I'm going in!' Ant launched the Shadow Knight towards the forest.

A few moments later he was surrounded by waving fronds of seagrass in a dim green twilight. It felt strange and spooky, as if undersea ghosts might be lurking in the shadows. But there were no ghosts in there, he told himself.

Only Edwina.

CHAPTER NINE

Ant penetrated further into the forest. The swirling seagrass closed behind him like a curtain. The tall fronds towered over his head, blotting out the light. He looked back at the way he'd come, but all he could see was a deep green darkness full of swaying shapes; he was already unsure if that was the way he'd come. All directions looked the same. *I'm lost*, he realised. *And I'm on my own.*

A finger of dread touched his heart.

And then his heart nearly burst out of his chest as a face suddenly peered through the grass at him.

Edwina parted the fronds and emerged in front of him. She hovered in the water, her tail gently rotating. She was smiling.

'Won't you come into my parlour, said the spider to the fly.'

Her words came through loud and clear. Her radio must be tuned to the same frequency as the Nektons' radio. I was right. She's been able to hear our radio messages all this time. How much did she know? Had she heard about the etching of the snake on the stonefish's lair? Ant was certain it was a clue to something. The glowing image on the Circlotron had confirmed that there was a link between the symbol on the stonefish's lair and their journey. He didn't want Edwina gatecrashing.

He tried to make his voice sound big and

bold and brave. 'What do you want?'

'You know what I want. The Circlotron, as you call it, is rightfully mine. Just give it to me and you won't get hurt.'

'Yeah, like I'm just going to hand it over!' He wished he felt as confident as he sounded. And he wished Fontaine was with him. He could use an ally right now.

'I know it's in your backpack,' said Edwina. 'Strange, isn't it, the way you keep turning up in front of me with the Circlotron? Almost like you want me to have it!'

Edwina was slowly moving closer. Ant saw the greed and excitement in her eyes.

I have to get out of here. I should never have come. Thinking quickly, he switched on the boosters on his Shadow Knight and shot upwards.

But Edwina reacted fast. Her metallic tail whirred and she shot up alongside him. She flipped on its end like a circus acrobat and

her tail scythed round, slicing through the Jorange's straps.

Ant's backpack tumbled down to the depths of the ocean, with Jeffrey spinning in his tank, flapping his fins helplessly.

Edwina dived after the Jorange.

But before she could reach it, a large white shape powered into view, leaving a trail of bubbles in its wake. With a stab of relief, Ant saw Fontaine in her White Knight scoop up the Jorange, a second before Edwina got there.

Once again Fontaine had arrived in the nick of time. She was never going to let him forget this.

Ant swam down to join her. The two of them stood side by side in their Knight suits, facing Edwina.

'Think you can take us both on?' said Fontaine.

'Yeah, and we have the Aronnax as backup!' said Ant. 'Why don't you just give up?'

Kaiko's voice came through on the radio. 'Need some help?'

'No, I think we've got this,' said Ant, not taking his eyes off Edwina.

Edwina's face behind her mask glowered with rage and frustration. She raised her hand and muttered into a wristwatch device on the sleeve of her selkie suit.

Ant looked at Fontaine. 'Who's she talking to?'

'You kids can have this round,' Edwina said. 'Enjoy it while you can. The next one will have a very different outcome, I can promise you that.'

Ant heard a rushing sound – and a moment later the Outcast homed in like a guided missile and came to a stop beside Edwina. A section of its gleaming titanium shell opened and Edwina climbed in.

'She must've radioed The Outcast,' said Ant to Fontaine.

'And it's a sub too!' Fontaine replied, unable to hide how impressed she was.

'I'll see you again,' Edwina said, staring out at them. The section of metallic lid closed over her, and the Outcast zoomed away.

Fontaine handed Ant the Jorange. He smiled in at Jeffrey, who swam up close to the glass, his mouth opening and closing as if to say 'Thank you!'

'What's that, Jeffrey?' Ant asked. 'I'm your hero? Well, you know I would never let you down, don't you?'

'Sorry to interrupt this touching reunion,' said Fontaine, 'but do you think we could get back to the Aronnax now? Or would you prefer to rush off and do something stupid all on your own again? Like go and pick a fight with a killer whale?'

'All right, all right,' Ant said. 'Let's go. Oh, and Fontaine ...'

'Yes?'

'Thanks.'

Fontaine smiled. 'All part of the service, little bro.'

*

The Nektons sat on the roof of the Aronnax, each of them sipping from a steaming mug of hot chocolate as they gathered for a debrief.

After Ant and Fontaine had clambered back through the Moon Pool, Kaiko had brought the Aronnax up to float on the surface of the ocean. It was a calm, mild night and the stars twinkled above them.

'That was all a bit hectic,' Will said. 'But we came through it – Edwina didn't get the Circlotron. We'd better keep it safe from now on.' He looked meaningfully at Ant.

'Yeah, OK,' said Ant, slightly shamefaced. 'Still ...' He brightened up. 'That was one cool adventure! We got the Circlotron back, and saved Jeffrey – and saw that amazing giant stonefish – and – and –'

Kaiko smiled at his excitement. 'We still have some unsolved mysteries on our hands though. How did Edwina know about the Circlotron?'

'Who else knew, apart from us?' asked Will.

Ant remembered how the pirate captain of the Dark Orca had seen inside his Jorange when he and Fontaine had been on their ship. 'Captain Hammerhead,' he said in a low, regretful voice.

'But why would he just give away information like that?' Fontaine asked.

'He might not give it away, but he'd definitely sell it,' said Will.

Back below deck, Kaiko nibbled a cookie thoughtfully. 'Edwina must have had the whole thing planned. It must have been her who jammed our satellite connection – she obviously has access to some pretty advanced technology. And when I was fixing the ballast tanks I saw they'd been sealed shut with a soldering iron. Remember when we felt that bumping under the hull? I bet that's when she did it.'

'And then she deliberately smashed into us during the storm – trying to damage the Aronnax so we'd have to stop for repairs!' added Ant.

'Well, her plan failed,' said Will. 'We still have the Circlotron.' It was now safely perched on the map table again, next to the Ephemychron.

'And Jeffrey!' Ant had placed the Jorange beside him, and Jeffrey was now happily nibbling at some fish food.

Suddenly Ant remembered the carving they'd seen outside the stonefish's lair. He jumped up and took the Circlotron from the map table. He spun it around in his palm, searching for the image of the serpent. And there it was, etched into the ring: the exact same sinuous curving shape, with the

protruding forked tongue and the small dot beside it.

'Look!' he said excitedly. 'It's here! I found this picture at the king's lair, etched into the stone!' He held the Circlotron out for his parents to see.

'I spotted it first!' said Fontaine.

'All right, *we* found it, then,' Ant conceded. 'What do you make of it, Dad?'

Will put on his glasses and scrutinised the image. 'It's right next to the etching of the Child of the Mountain,' he said. 'And then when you get to the stonefish's lair, you find an image of a snake – so now we just need to work out where it's leading us.'

'It's like – it's leading us along a route,' Fontaine said. 'First the dragon's cave – then the stonefish's lair –'

'There's only one way to find out!' Ant took the Circlotron from his dad and pressed his hands against its curved sides.

It still amazed him to think that he was the only Nekton who could summon the Circlotron to life. Instantly a powerful beam of white light shot up into the sky. It traced a path through the stars, arcing towards the west.

'It's pointing in the direction of the Indian Ocean,' Kaiko said.

At the same moment the etching of the snake began to glow.

'There's something familiar about that shape ...' said Will.

He pulled out a map. He unfolded it on the floor and they all crouched around it. Will traced the course of a winding blue river with his finger. 'It's the Pangani River,' he said. 'See? It's the same shape.'

'Where is the Pangani River?' asked Ant.

'In Africa,' Will said, straightening up to gaze across the water. 'It flows through Tanzania.'

'And its mouth is in the Indian Ocean,' said Kaiko.

There was a pause as they all looked at each other.

'I reckon we know where we're going, then,' said Will.

Ant leaped to his feet and pointed dramatically in the same direction as the Circlotron's beam. 'Nektons – set sail!'

'Well, tomorrow,' said Kaiko. 'Let's have a good night's sleep first.' She began to walk over to the control deck. 'I'll key in the coordinates, ready to set off at sunrise. '

Will rolled up his map. They all began to move down the hallway towards their bedrooms.

A short while later, lying in bed, Ant tossed and turned, struggling to get to sleep. He couldn't rid himself of the thought that Edwina was out there somewhere.

'This isn't over,' he whispered to himself.

'Not by a long way.' If the Nektons were going to follow the route mapped out by the Circlotron, there were two big questions still to be answered.

Did Edwina know, or could she guess, where the Aronnax was heading to next?

And what would they find when they got there?

THE SEA IS DEEP
AND FULL OF SECRETS

TURN OVER TO FIND OUT MORE!

DID YOU READ THE NEKTONS' FIRST ADVENTURE IN

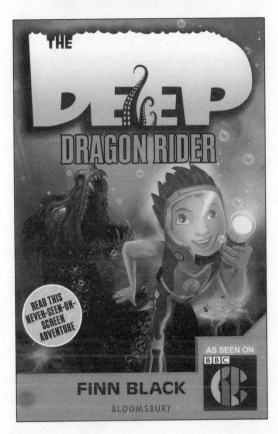

PROLOGUE

'**C**ome on, Jeffrey! Last one there's a blobfish!'

Ant Nekton zoomed through the ocean in the Shadow Knight, the sleek, high-tech underwater exploration suit he used for missions. Beside his visor, he could see Jeffrey, his pet fish – and best friend – flapping his fins furiously to keep up, but the Shadow Knight was too fast for him. Ant steered the suit down to the sea bed and away from the

Aronnax, the giant submarine that the Nekton family called home, which floated above them like a huge metal whale.

Ant had convinced his parents, Will and Kaiko, to let him explore the nearby kelp forests. As a junior explorer, he knew that the kelp forests were often used by organisms as a safe place to hide from predators. Ant was always on the lookout for new discoveries, whether it was a strange species of sea snail, or something more exciting ...

As he approached the forest he cut the Knight's engines so that the vibrations fell to a low hum. He didn't want to disturb any forms of sea life living there. He felt his heart give a nervous flutter. There was no telling what he might find in the depths of the ocean ...

'OK, what do we have today?' he muttered. Jeffrey finally caught up and swam next to Ant, his eyes bulging from the effort. If a fish could pant for breath, that's what Jeffrey would have been doing. Ant reached out the Knight's mechanical hands to part the swaying column of kelp and peered between the strands. 'Kelp ... kelp ... and more kelp. Hmm, I was hoping for something a little less ... *kelpy*.'

They investigated a little further and found nothing more than a strangely coloured piece of algae, but then Jeffrey darted off towards a hidden corner of the forest.

'Jeffrey? What is it? Have you found something?'

Ant followed his little orange and purple fish to a mound of sand and looked closely at it.

'Seems like it's just a heap of sand,' he said to his faithful fish. 'Come on, let's go back to – *Whoa*!'

A sudden swell of current buffeted the Shadow Knight and caused the kelp forest to sway. Grain by grain, the sand mound in front of them drifted away to reveal a strange, ancient-looking object beneath the surface.

Ant felt his eyes grow wide and his skin prickle. 'What. Is. *That?!*'

He carefully brushed away the rest of the sand to reveal a round metal object the size of a cricket ball. It was a dirty green, the colour of an old, unpolished penny. Around the centre of the sphere was a protruding ring, and it was covered in barnacle shells, just as most things were under the sea when they had been there for a long time. But how long? Something about the look of it made Ant think it had been there for centuries.

Slowly, he lifted the orb out of its resting place and instantly felt a shiver of excitement run down his body. Jeffrey danced around him.

'It could be anything.' Ant shrugged. 'Maybe just a piece of sea junk, or something someone dropped off the side of their boat years ago.' He glanced at Jeffrey and burst out in a grin. 'Who am I kidding? I have no idea what this is, but it's definitely *awesome*!'

It wasn't every day that Ant came across buried treasure in a kelp forest.

He held it gently in his mechanical grip and powered up the Shadow Knight. He turned to head back to the Aronnax, where he would be able to investigate properly.

'Jeffrey, old pal, I have a feeling life in the ocean just became even *more* interesting ...'

A column of bubbles erupted from the little fish as he mouthed his agreement. The two of them headed home. This discovery was something they *had* to share ... when Ant was ready.

CHAPTER ONE

'**Y**ou guys are not going to *believe* this!'

Ant carried his mystery object across the bridge of the Aronnax. The orb was covered with an old dust sheet. He'd managed to keep his discovery a secret from the rest of the Nektons for an entire two weeks while he'd worked on it. None of them had any idea it even existed.

It was nearly dusk and the family had just returned from a talk Kaiko had given at the Tokyo University of Marine Science. Everyone, that is, except Ant, who had stayed behind to prepare his surprise. Ant loved visiting new places but, having grown up on a submarine, being on solid land felt peculiar to him. There wasn't the usual hum of engines and swaying movement that he was so used to on the Aronnax.

Ant carefully placed the strange object on a control panel.

'So what have we got here, Ant?' asked Will. The Nektons gathered round, used to Ant's hobby of creating imaginative (and occasionally unsuccessful) inventions.

'You remember that I went exploring in the kelp forests a while ago?' he began, looking from face to face. He paused for dramatic effect. 'I found something!'

'Would that "something" be the reason you stayed back on board the Aronnax these past couple of weeks?' said Kaiko with a smile and a raised eyebrow. 'I thought you said you were staying behind to "guard" the Aronnax?'

'Um, I was kind of doing both?' said Ant

with a sheepish grin. 'I've been working on restoring my "something" to its former glory. And now I want you all to see it!'

'Can't this wait, son?' yawned Will. 'I think we're all pretty beat from your mother's talk at the university – which was excellent, by the way, dear!'

'Thank you!' smiled Kaiko, folding her arms. 'Good to know I didn't bore you to sleep.'

'What is so important that it has to keep me from my bed?' said Ant's sister, Fontaine, giving him a level stare.

'Trust me,' said Ant, 'this'll be worth it.'

The family looked on in anticipation.

'Ladies and gentlemen! And you, Fontaine! I am pleased to finally unveil the latest of my amazing, mind-boggling, awe-inducing discoveries!' Ant performed a drum roll on his tummy. 'I call it – the CIRCLOTRON!'

He whipped the dust sheet away to reveal the strange-looking contraption he had saved from the sea bed. Since recovering it, Ant had lovingly cleaned it and carefully brushed away the mud of hundreds, maybe thousands of years, so that it was now a tarnished brown colour.

'The ... *Circlotron*?' said Fontaine, peering at it.

'Yeah!'

'Seriously?'

'Yeah, seriously!' said Ant, affronted. 'It didn't have a name, so Jeffrey and I came up with one. Cool, huh?'

Fontaine rolled her eyes.

'I'm going to bed,' she said, turning to leave.

'Wait a second, Fontaine,' said Will. He moved closer to inspect the unusual device. 'Your brother may have something here. What does it do, Ant?'

'Do?' said Ant. 'Um ... I haven't got a clue! But that's the fun part about science, right?

Finding out about stuff?'

'It certainly is,' said Kaiko, peering at the Circlotron. 'What are those markings?' She traced her fingers over a few engravings on the ring that ran around the centre of the globe.

'They're glyphs. Lemurian, wouldn't you say, Dad?' said Ant.

Will grinned as he examined the Circlotron more closely. 'If this is a Lemurian artefact, then it is incredibly exciting.'

'Look – just yesterday I cleared away some impacted sand and I found this hole in the side.' Ant angled the Circlotron so that the others could see a tiny hole, hidden beneath the ring. 'I think it might be a keyhole. Maybe it's mechanical, like clockwork?'

'And you want to wind it up?' said Fontaine. 'It could be anything! A crazy, mechanical cricket ball! A weird robot-fish egg!'

'*Or* it could be the next clue to discovering the ancient city of Lemuria! What do you think,

Dad?' Ant looked at Will hopefully.

Will donned his reading glasses to look at the symbols and walked around the Circlotron for a few moments, stroking his chin in thought. Will had dedicated his entire life to researching the lost, ancient civilisation of Lemuria, and no one knew more on the subject than him.

'The symbols are definitely Lemurian,' he admitted. 'Are you sure this is going to work, Ant?'

'Come on, Dad! When has anything I've done ever gone wrong?' said Ant. Will drew breath to speak. 'Actually, don't answer that! This is *totally* going to work.'

Will and Kaiko looked at each other and shrugged.

'Let's do it!'

Will fetched some tools and managed to bend a piece of metal to fit the shape of the keyhole. Ant scooped up the Circlotron into the palm of his hand. Then, shaking with excitement, he took the key and slid it into the Circlotron. He turned it and to his surprise there was no resistance – it smoothly went round. From deep inside the Circlotron they could hear a series of whirrs and cracks and clicks. Cogs which had laid unused for centuries began to move. He felt a judder travel through his hand as the device buzzed into life.

'Nektons,' said Ant with an air of drama, 'meet the Circlotron.' The ball hummed and whirred and suddenly a shaft of white light shot out from the top, making Ant almost drop it – almost.

'Whoa!' said Fontaine.

'Yes! It worked!' Ant held out the Circlotron. He could feel its energy pulsing through him. Will and Kaiko moved out of the way of the beam, shielding their eyes.

'Aargh! Put it down!' shouted Fontaine,

dazzled by the light. 'Did you find an ancient Lemurian flashlight?'

'What? No! Whatever this is, it's *way* more important than a flashlight.' Ant placed the Circlotron carefully on the floor. The light seemed to settle and point upwards, through the observation window and into the night sky. The beam moved wildly west to east.

'Really? Because it looks like a flashlight,' said Fontaine, not even trying to hide a yawn. 'I'll be in my room ...'

Ant stared at the light and the path it cut into the sky. Whatever this was, he knew it was essential to understanding the Lemurians. He could feel it in his bones. He looked up at the light and tried to track where the line was pointing. Suddenly –

'Oh. Oh, whoa! I think ... I think I know ...' Ant stumbled over his words as a hundred thoughts hit him at once. 'I think I know what it does!'

Still holding the Circlotron in the palm of his hand, Ant rushed to a control panel to note down the current coordinates of the Aronnax and started to do some mental calculations. He grabbed a tablet computer and brought up a map of their position. *Yes!* he thought. *It fits!*

As the beam of light moved, it was drawing a straight line through the black pit of space, highlighting several stars along its path. 'I've got it! We're travelling towards the equator, which is to the south, here,' he said, pointing to the on-screen map. 'Look at the line the light is pointing to. The Circlotron must be tracking the *celestial* equator!'

'Remarkable,' said Will.

'You're right! Very clever, Ant!' said Kaiko. She gave her son a hug. Fontaine looked at her family and shrugged.

'I don't get it,' she said. 'What's the big deal?'

'It's –' began Will.

'Dad, allow me,' said Ant with a grin. 'I don't mind explaining to my sister.'

Fontaine rolled her eyes, but she was listening.

Ant paced across the floor as he explained. 'The celestial equator is just like it says. The equator is an imaginary line around the middle of the Earth, right? Well, the *celestial* equator is an imaginary line across the night sky.'

'Er ... right,' said Fontaine.

'Say you got a rubber band and stretched it around the world,' he said.

'That's a pretty *big* rubber band!' Fontaine laughed.

'Well, if you keep stretching it outwards, that's the celestial equator. The Circlotron is tracking it and projecting it on to the sky. Look!' Ant pointed to the bright beam of light. 'See how that glowing white line runs through the constellations? Right above us, the line goes straight through Mintaka – the rightmost star in Orion's Belt!'

Fontaine nodded, finally grasping the concept.

'I ... I *suppose* that's pretty cool ...' she mumbled. Ant leaped up again and Will ruffled his hair.

'Good job, son,' he said. 'You've been studying the stars, haven't you?'

'A little,' Ant shrugged modestly. In truth, he had been reading up on constellations and astronomy for months. 'I just thought that the more I understood about how the skies and the oceans connect, the closer we might get to discovering where Lemuria is located.'

'Great thinking,' nodded Will. 'After all, we know that the ancient Lemurians used the stars as their guide across the seas. It could be that the Circlotron – *love* the name, by the way – is an ancient piece of Lemurian maritime equipment.'

Ant smiled. Finding the lost city of Lemuria was the Nekton family's mission, and Ant loved doing anything he could to help. He stared into the night sky, daydreaming about finally finding Lemuria. He was smugly congratulating himself on his discovery when –

WOOP WOOP WOOP!

The shrill sound made Ant jump. A call was coming through, the Aronnax's monitors flashing red. He placed the Circlotron back down and the whirring sound from within stopped. The cogs inside ground to a halt and the light faded. Ant went to his position on the bridge, where Kaiko and Will were already in their seats.

'It's an emergency call from the Worldwide Oceanic Association!' said Will. 'They need our help – now!'

THE SEA IS FULL OF SECRETS!

Join the Nektons on their daring underwater
adventures with more books all about

NEVER SEEN ON SCREEN!

THE DEEP:
STICKER ACTIVITY BOOK

The Nekton family are on a mission to
shine light on the darkest extremes of the
ocean. Packed with super submersibles,
astonishing sea creatures and breathtaking
Lemurian mysteries, this sticker activity
book will take you on all the amazing
aquatic adventures of The Deep!

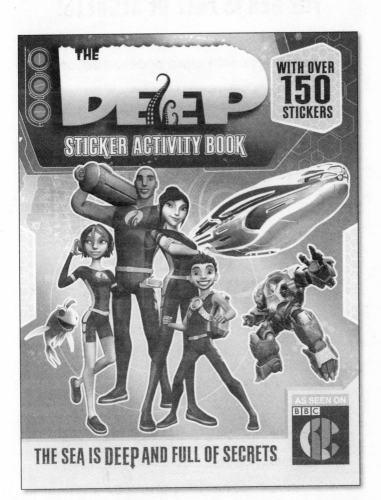

THE SEA IS FULL OF SECRETS!

Join the Nektons on their daring underwater

adventures with more books all about

NEVER SEEN ON SCREEN!

THE DEEP:
THE OFFICIAL HANDBOOK

Explore the depths of the captivating world

of The Deep with this official handbook,

the must-have companion to the hit TV

series! It's packed with never-seen-before

material, including in-depth profiles of all

your favourite characters and behind-the-

scenes stories that have inspired episodes.

Discover the secrets of Lemuria and watch

out for pirates along the way!

TURN OVER FOR SOME FUN GAMES!

CORAL AND CURRENTS

Fontaine is roaming the ocean in the White Knight, searching for a rare species of hermit crab. Now it's time to return to the Aronnax. Can you help her find a way through this rocky reef? Kaiko is worried – Fontaine's air supply is running low!

THE WHITE KNIGHT

The White Knight is a single-person, armoured diving suit. It can reach places underwater that would be too difficult for a normal diver to explore.

THE SEA IS THE KEY

The Nektons are determined to find the sunken city of Lemuria, even if it takes years! All they have to guide them are a few ancient artefacts. Study these four Lemurian symbols. The same sequence only appears once on the tablet below. Can you find it?

PROTEUS

Proteus is the leader of the Guardians, a secret society who have existed for thousands of years. They are tasked with protecting Lemuria and its treasures.

Got it right? Proteus will be impressed! Stick the Guardian in here.

7

LOOK OUT FOR MORE ADVENTURES FROM

COMING IN 2019!